Fame Thing

by

Jonathan Meres

First published in 2006 in Great Britain by
Barrington Stoke Ltd
www.barringtonstoke.co.uk

Copyright © 2006 Jonathan Meres

The moral right of the author has been asserted in
accordance with the Copyright, Designs and
Patents Act 1988

ISBN-10: 1-84299-370-4
ISBN-13: 978-1-84299-370-5

Printed in Great Britain by Bell & Bain Ltd

For Hamish

Contents

A Note from the Author

I'd just finished writing this book when George Best died. George Best was one of the most famous footballers ever. He was a hero to kids like me, who were growing up in the 1970s. He was like David Beckham and Wayne Rooney rolled into one!

If someone had ever told me that George Best was moving into my village, I wouldn't have believed them in a million years! It was amazing enough – and this is true – when I was given a book signed by George and the rest of the Manchester United team. "To Jonathan," it said. "Best wishes, George Best."

I've still got it. And it still means the world to me. Even if I *do* support Nottingham Forest! (Come on you Reds, by the way!) Why am I telling you this? Well, you'll just have to read *Fame Thing* and find out, won't you?

Chapter 1
Name Thing

The school bus drove off. George and her brother Denis were alone. It was a warm spring afternoon. Birds sang in the trees. The old church clock struck four. But George had only one thing on her mind.

"Well?" she said.

"Well what?" said her brother, Denis.

"Who do you think's going to win tonight?"

Denis let out a long sigh.

"I have no idea who's going to win tonight, George. And do you know something? I couldn't care less."

George looked up at Denis from her wheelchair.

"Are you serious?"

"I've never been more serious in my life," said Denis.

"No, but really."

"Really, George. I couldn't care less."

"But it's the semi-final replay, Den! You've *got* to care!"

"Have I? Why's that then?"

"Because ... because ..." said George. "Because you just have to, that's all!"

Denis laughed.

"What's so funny?"

"You, George. You're funny."

"I don't see what's so funny about liking football."

"Liking football?" said Denis. "*Liking* football? You're obsessed with it! That's all you think about!"

"So?" said George. "What's wrong with that?"

Denis rolled his eyes. She just didn't get it. She just couldn't get her head round the fact that he'd sooner watch paint dry than watch a football match.

"There's nothing wrong with it," said Denis.

"Anyway, it's not my fault," George went on.

"So whose fault is it, then?" Denis wanted to know.

"Dad's," said George.

"Dad's?"

"Yeah, well, he's the one who named me after a famous footballer, isn't he?"

"He named *me* after a famous footballer as well," said Denis. "And I *hate* football."

Denis didn't like anyone to know why he was called Denis. He'd been named after Denis Law, who'd played for Manchester United way back when his dad had been a kid. His sister George was named after George Best, another ex-United player and one of the most famous footballers ever. Her proper name wasn't really George, it was Georgina. But everyone called her George.

"So?" said George.

Denis didn't say anything. *If George wanted to have the last word*, he thought, *then fine, she could have it.* He started to push his sister along the pavement.

"Get a move on!" said George. "I can go faster than this myself!"

But Denis just smiled. He knew she was kidding.

"Oi, Georgie!" yelled a voice from across the road.

George turned around. It was her best friend Nick's dad.

"What's the score going to be tonight then?" Nick's dad shouted over.

Denis shook his head. What was it with these people? Hadn't they got better things to think about?

"Chelsea," yelled George. "3-1 after extra time."

"What? So now you can predict the future?" said Denis to his sister.

George didn't reply. She'd seen a huge removals lorry. It roared past them and rumbled round the corner.

"Did you see that?" said George.

"Yeah," said Denis. "A removals lorry. What about it?"

"It must be going to The Elms."

"Great," said Denis, trying not to yawn.

"I wonder who it is then?" said George. "They reckon it might be someone famous."

"Dunno," said Denis. "You tell me. You're the one with special powers."

"Ha ha. Very funny," said George.

Chapter 2
You're Kidding!

It had been the talk of the village for months. Who was going to move into The Elms?

The Elms was the biggest house for miles around. It had a swimming pool and tennis court, as well as huge sweeping lawns and a lake.

The house itself was very old. It had at least ten bedrooms. And there was a library and a ballroom and a hallway full of suits of armour.

Ever since the "For Sale" sign had been taken down and the "Sold" sign had gone up, all anyone wanted to talk about was *who had bought the Elms?*

Some people said it was someone famous. Some said it was a pop star. Others said it might be an actor.

Some people in the village said they didn't want any showbiz types moving in. Others thought it would be brilliant. After all, this was a place where the closest thing to a celebrity was some guy who'd been an extra in EastEnders.

"I think they should turn The Elms into something useful, like an old folks' home," said George's mum, as she was giving George and Denis their tea.

"So do I, Mum," said Denis. "There's something wrong about one person living in a place that big when there's homeless people on the streets."

"What are you on about?" said George. "Are you telling me you wouldn't buy a place like that if you could afford it?"

"Correct," said Denis.

"You liar!" said George.

"Come on you two, stop it and eat up," said Mum.

"Have you got a big envelope, Mum?" said George.

"Why?" asked Mum.

"So we can send all our left-overs to the starving children in Africa."

"God, you're so immature sometimes, George," said Denis.

But before George could reply, her mobile rang. It was her best friend, Nick.

"Hello?" she said. "Oh hi, Nick, how's it going?"

George paused. "You're kidding!" she said.

George's mum and Denis looked at each other. What could have happened?

"You have *got* to be kidding!" screeched George into her mobile.

"What is it?" said Denis, but George just ignored him.

"If this is your idea of a joke, Nick Watson, I'm going to ..."

George stopped talking and listened.

"You've *seen* him?" she said.

"Who?" said Denis.

"Are you sure it was him?" said George, ignoring her mum and her brother.

"Who?" yelled Denis and Mum together.

"I'll be round in a few minutes!" said George. "Yeah. Bye!"

George put her phone back in her pocket.

"You're *never* going to guess who's moved into the Elms," she said.

"You're right. We never are, so why don't you just tell us?" said Denis.

"Only Dean flipping Johnson, that's who!" said George.

"Dean Johnson?" said George's mum. "Do you mean the footballer?"

George looked at her mother as if she'd just stepped off a spaceship.

"Is there *another* Dean Johnson, Mum? Of course I mean the footballer!"

"He's very young, isn't he?" said George's mum.

"Yeah. And very stupid," said Denis.

"You're just jealous," said George.

"What? Jealous of a guy with the brain of a snail?" said Denis. "I don't think so!"

"For someone who hates football, you seem to know an awful lot about it," said George.

"Dean Johnson's never out of the papers!" said Denis. "Everyone knows about him. There's a new story every day!"

"Are you going round to Nick's, then, George?" said her mum.

"Do you mind, Mum?"

"Do I have a choice?" asked Mum.

"Not really, no," said George, with a grin.

"Go on, then."

"Thanks, Mum."

There was a moment's pause. George looked at her brother and smiled.

"Denis?"

Denis knew what she was going to ask.

"Any chance of a push?" George said.

"I thought you said you can go faster by yourself?"

George fluttered her eyelashes.

"Pleeeeeeeeease?"

Denis looked at his mum.

"Go on. Clear off, the pair of you," sighed George's mum. "I'll put your tea in the oven."

"Thanks, Mum," said Denis.

"I owe you one, Den," said George.

"You owe me more than one," said Denis, pushing his sister towards the door.

George smiled.

"That was rotten, what you said just then," she said to Denis as he pushed her down the road.

13

"What? You mean about Dean Johnson having the brain of a snail?" said Denis.

"It was offensive."

"Yeah. To *snails*," said Denis.

"I'll get you!" said George.

"You'll have to catch me first," laughed Denis.

Chapter 3

The Boy with the Golden Feet

Dean Johnson had only just turned 16 when he became the youngest ever player to score a goal in the Premiership. And what a goal it had been. An absolute screamer from the edge of the box. The goalie had stood no chance. The crowd went mad. Right there, right then, a star was born.

Dean proved he wasn't just a one-hit wonder when he scored another goal in the next match. In fact, he scored five goals in his first seven matches. And they were all fantastic. Volleys, long-range shots, diving headers, the lot! Dean didn't seem to score ordinary, boring sorts of goals. He left those to the other players.

A buzz went through the crowd whenever Dean got the ball. They expected him to score, or at the very least, do something exciting. Dean didn't disappoint. More often than not, he delivered the goods. The fans chanted his name. He was the new football god.

It was true that Dean Johnson wasn't the smartest guy on the block. He wasn't what you'd call rocket scientist material. But then, he didn't want to *be* a rocket scientist. The only thing Dean Johnson had ever wanted to do was play football. And boy, could Dean Johnson play football!

The newspapers went Dean crazy. He was never off the back pages. They all called Dean "Deano". It was Deano this, Deano that and Deano the other. It seemed that Dean could do no wrong. Nobody had a bad word to say about him. Kids loved him. Mums and dads loved him. Grannies loved him. Everybody loved him.

Everyone agreed. Dean Johnson was The Boy With The Golden Feet.

For a while, all went well. Dean became both super-famous and super-rich. He soon had more money than he knew what to do with. More money than sense, some people said. But Dean didn't care. He bought his first Ferrari when he was still too young to drive it. He bought his second one just after.

Before long Dean began to appear in advertisements. His face was on everything, from hair gel and deodorant to soft drinks and instant noodles.

Dean wasn't what you'd call handsome. But that didn't stop girls fancying him all of a sudden. Girls who wouldn't have looked at him twice before.

Was it because they knew, in their heart of hearts, that beauty is only skin deep? That looks aren't everything?

No. It was because Dean Johnson was rich and famous. Even Dean could see that. But he wasn't bothered. He was having way too much fun to be bothered. If the girls were shallow, that was their problem, not his. If they were only interested in him because he was loaded, that was fine by Dean.

So Dean Johnson spent the next few months being the centre of attention and loving every minute of it. He went to all the best shows and all the most glitzy parties. He rubbed shoulders with rock stars, film stars and even politicians. And the weird thing was, *they* all wanted to be seen with *Dean*, not the other way round.

And then it happened. A row in a nightclub. Too much to drink. Jealous boyfriends and crying girlfriends. Raised voices and raised fists. A scuffle. Punches thrown.

A photographer from a tabloid newspaper just happened to be there. Some people said it was all a set-up. That the people in the fight had been offered money. By the photographer.

Whatever the truth was, the nightclub punch-up led to Dean Johnson's first ever bit of bad press.

"CLUBBING DEANO IN DRUNKEN BRAWL!!" the headlines screamed. And underneath was a photo of Dean, grabbing someone by the scruff of the neck.

There were plenty more Deano headlines after that. And none of them good.

"DEANO'S NIGHT OF SHAME!" said one.

"DEANO DECKS DAVE!" said another, after Dean had hit someone for having the nerve to ask for an autograph.

And just like that, the tide had turned. It was the end of Dean Johnson's all too short honeymoon period with his adoring public. No longer The Boy With The Golden Feet, Dean was now an out of control, foul-mouthed, overpaid, drunken idiot.

Everyone agreed. Dean Johnson had grown too big for his golden boots.

Well, the newspapers said he had, anyway.

Chapter 4

Question Time

George started asking questions before Nick had even opened the door.

"So what's he like then? Did you say anything to him? Did he see you? Did he say anything to you? What's he like? Come on! I'm waiting!"

George stopped, but only because she'd run out of breath. Nick thought for a moment.

"OK, for a start, no, I *don't* know what he's like. No, I *didn't* say anything to him, and no, he *didn't* say anything to me."

Nick paused.

"Oh and I don't know if he *saw* me because he just drove right past. He might have done. But I'm not sure. Amazing car by the way. Red Ferrari!"

George looked fed up.

"Hi, Nick," said Denis loudly.

"Hi, Denis," replied Nick.

"Look, I'd love to stop, I really would," said Denis, as he began to head back down the path. "Except I already have a life, thanks."

"Hey, look, *you* might not think this is a big deal," George shouted after him. "But it is! It's a *huge* deal!"

Denis shrugged.

"Whatever," he said.

"Don't give me that 'whatever' rubbish, Den!" said George. "'Whatever' is what people say when they know they're wrong!"

Denis shrugged again.

"Whatever," he said, setting off back down the street.

George thought about yelling something else, but didn't. There were more important matters to attend to.

"So are we going to go round there or what?" she said.

"What? You mean and just hang around outside the gates like a couple of saddoes?" said Nick.

"Exactly," said George.

"Sounds good to me," said Nick.

23

"Excellent," said George. "Give us a push then."

The questions began again as soon as they set off.

"So what did he look like?" George asked.

"Just like he looks on the telly," said Nick.

"Did he have anyone with him? Like a girl or anything?"

"I don't think so, no. Why?"

"Nothing," said George. "No reason. I just wondered, that's all."

Nick didn't say anything, but when George turned round to look at him, she could see that he was smiling.

"What?" said George.

"You fancy him, don't you?"

"Eh? What are you on about? Course I don't fancy him!"

24

"So how come you're going red?"

"I'm not going red!" protested George. But she knew that she was.

"Yeah, you are," said Nick. "You fancy him, I know you do."

"I do not!"

Nick just smiled again.

"Stop smiling like that!"

"Like what?"

"Like that!"

Nick might have been George's best friend, but sometimes he drove her mad. *This* was one of those sometimes.

"It's OK if you *do* fancy him, George," he said.

"I didn't realise I needed your permission," said George. "But thanks anyway."

25

"That's not what I mean," said Nick. "I mean he's only four years older than you, isn't he? He's nineteen and you're fifteen."

"So?" said George.

"Well, my dad's four years older than my mum."

"So?" said George again, getting more and more annoyed.

"So it's understandable if you have feelings for him."

George took a deep breath. She was doing her best to stay cool.

"Nick?"

"Yeah?"

"I do *not* fancy Dean Johnson, all right?"

"Yeah, but I'm just saying that if you did ..."

"I do not fancy Dean Johnson!" yelled George. "Which part of that do you not understand?"

"OK, OK!" said Nick.

"And even if I *did* ... which I *don't* ... he's not going to go out with someone like me, is he? I mean do I look like a footballer's girlfriend?"

"Er, not really, no," said Nick.

"Do I have dyed blonde hair?"

"No."

"Do I wear skirts up to my armpits?"

"No."

"Can I string more than two words together?"

"No. I mean, yes."

"Well then," said George. "I'm hurt, Nick, I really am. You think I'd fancy somebody just because they're famous and they've got loads of money? How stupid do you think I am?"

"Sorry," said Nick.

"That's OK." George paused. "It would be different if he was rich, famous *and* good looking," she said. "I'd be right in there!"

Nick laughed. "Oh come on, he's not *that* bad looking!" he said with a grin.

By now they'd arrived outside The Elms. Workmen were busy fitting electronic gates and CCTV cameras.

"Are those to help keep *us* out, or *him* in?" asked George.

"What d'you think he's really like?" said Nick. "D'you think it's all true? All that stuff in the papers?"

"Why don't you ask him?" said a voice.

George and Nick turned round.

It was Dean Johnson.

Chapter 5

When George Met Dean

George screamed. It was just such a shock to see Dean Johnson standing there. She'd seen him on telly millions of times and now here he was – right in front of her.

"Sorry. I didn't mean to scare you," said Dean.

"That's OK," croaked George.

"I'm Dean, by the way," he went on.

"Hi," George whispered.

"What's your name?"

"Erm ..."

George was still gob-smacked.

"Her name's George," said Nick. "After George Best."

"Georgie Best, eh?" said Dean. "He was some player."

"I'm Nick, by the way."

"Pleased to meet you, Nick," said Dean.

Nick and Dean shook hands.

"Pleased to meet you too, George," said Dean, holding out his hand.

"Pleased to meet you," said George, shaking it.

"Right, well, that's the formal stuff over with," said Dean. "Are you coming in or what?"

"Sorry?" said George.

31

Had she heard right? Was Dean Johnson really inviting them into his home? He couldn't be! He was one of the most famous people in the country! Why would he want to do a thing like that? It had to be some kind of mistake.

But it wasn't.

"I just thought you might like to come in or something?" said Dean. "Everything's still in boxes. But the TV's unpacked. And the match is about to start. I want to know who we're going to play in the final. I mean, you don't have to if you don't want to. But ..."

Dean never got to finish the sentence. Nick was already pushing George up the drive.

"I'll take that as a 'yes' then," said Dean, following them.

"What are you doing?" hissed George.

"What does it look like I'm doing?" said Nick.

"We can't do this!"

"We flipping well can!" said Nick.

"But he's a complete stranger!"

"No, he's not! He's Dean Johnson!"

"Yes, I know that," said George. "But ..."

"So what's this place like then?" said Dean, catching up with them.

"Oh, er, quiet," said George. "Very quiet."

"Yeah, that's what I thought," said Dean.

"You must have known that, though?"

"What?" said Dean. "Nah, not really. It's only the second time I've been here."

"Are you serious?" said Nick.

"Yeah."

"How come?"

"It's all been fixed up for me," said Dean. "Everything gets done. About the only thing I have to do myself is wipe my bum. And I'm pretty sure if I asked, they'd do that for me too."

"Who are 'they'?" said George.

"My people," said Dean.

"Your people? Makes you sound like Jesus or something."

"Jesus? Who does he play for?"

George hoped that Dean was joking. He couldn't be *that* stupid, could he? Or could he?

"What do you mean by 'your people'?" asked Nick.

"Agents, PR people, that kind of thing," said Dean. "There's loads of them."

"What do PR people do?" Nick asked.

"That's a good question," said Dean. "Not much, if you ask me. I should sack the lot of them."

"PR means Public Relations," explained George. "They deal with the press and all that."

"Oh, I see," said Nick.

By now they were at the house. The removals lorry George had seen before was outside. Men were busy running up and down a wooden ramp, like worker ants.

Nick started to push George up the ramp, but it was hard work.

"Come on, Nick!" teased George. "What are you? A girl or something?"

"Shut your face, you!" said Nick. "If you weren't such a porker – !"

"Here, let me," said Dean. He took over from Nick behind the wheelchair.

"Thanks," said George.

"Does your boyfriend always talk to you like that?" said Dean.

George looked horrified. "Nick? My boyfriend? Are you crazy?"

"Haven't you got a boyfriend, then?" asked Dean.

"I didn't say that, did I?" snapped George.

"I was just asking, that's all," said Dean.

"Why?" said George. "Have you got a girlfriend?"

"Depends," said Dean.

"What do you mean, it depends?"

"Depends which paper you read." Dean laughed.

George smiled. She was beginning to suspect that Dean Johnson wasn't quite so stupid after all.

Chapter 6
Fame Thing

The Elms was every bit as grand on the inside as it looked from the outside.

"Well? What do you think?" said Dean.

"It's amazing!" said Nick. "You could fit the whole of our house into this hallway!"

"Yeah, I know, it's mad isn't it?" said Dean.

"Good grief, look at that massive light!" said George. "You won't find one of those in B&Q!"

Dean laughed.

"If you think *that's* over the top, you should see the one in my bedroom!" he said.

Nick looked at George and smiled. George glared back at Nick.

"Anyone fancy a drink?" said Dean. "I could murder a Coke!"

"Yeah, that would be great, thanks," said George.

"Excuse me, mate," said Dean to one of the removals men. "Which way is it to the kitchen?"

"Down there, past the dining room, along the corridor, first on the right. You can't miss it," said the removals man.

"Cheers, mate," said Dean.

"You mean you've not been to the kitchen before?" said Nick.

"Oh I've *been* there," said Dean. "I just can't remember how to *get* there."

"This place is unreal," said George.

"My whole life is unreal," said Dean. "Come on, let's go."

They set off. Dean pushed George's wheelchair and Nick followed behind.

"So, who do you fancy then?" said Dean.

George couldn't believe it. She'd only known Dean Johnson for a few minutes and already he was asking her who she fancied! How dare he?

"Well?" said Dean.

"I beg your pardon?" said George.

"Who do you fancy? To win tonight?"

"Oh, right! You mean the *match*," said George. "Er, Chelsea. 3-1 after extra time. What do you reckon?"

"Yeah, Chelsea. 2-0," said Dean. "Don't think it'll go as far as extra time."

"What about the final?" said George. "Do you think you'll win?"

Dean smiled.

"Do you want a Coke or not?" he said.

"Yeah, shut up, George!" said Nick. "I think you'll win, Dean. No problem."

"Cheers, mate. I hope you're right," said Dean. "Hey, look, we've made it!"

They were in the kitchen. It was huge. Just like everything else in the house. Dean headed for the fridge, opened the door and took out three cans of Coke.

"Here you go," he said. He handed a can each to George and Nick.

"Thanks, Dean," said Nick.

"Yeah, thanks," said George.

They all opened their cans and had a drink.

"This is crazy," said George.

"What is?" said Dean.

"Us being here," said George. "With you."

"What's so crazy about that?" said Dean.

"You're Dean Johnson!" said George.

"Yeah, I know I am," said Dean. "So what?"

"You're famous!"

"What's that got to do with anything? Am I only allowed to mix with other famous people or something?"

Dean was smiling, but George had a feeling that he wasn't joking.

"I never asked to be famous, you know," Dean went on. "I never even *wanted* to be famous. I just wanted to play football, that's all. And now I do. It's my job. And I happen to get paid shedloads of money for doing it. I'm just lucky. I mean, look at this place! I

don't belong here! I'm nineteen years old!
I'm just a normal bloke! This time last year I
was still living in a council house with my
mum!"

"Sorry," said George.

"Why? What's wrong with my mum?" said
Dean, smiling.

"No, I meant sorry about the fame thing,"
said George. "It must do your head in."

"Tell me about it," said Dean. "I mean,
don't get me wrong. Sometimes it can be
great. But other times it can be a right pain."

They all took another gulp of Coke.

"I shouldn't be drinking this stuff," said
Dean, patting his stomach. "Got to watch the
old weight and all that."

"Oh, I don't know. You look all right to
me," said George.

Nick sniggered.

"What's up with you?" said George. "I just meant Dean doesn't need to watch his weight, that was all."

At that moment a mobile phone rang. It was Dean's. He answered it.

"Hello?" said Dean. "Oh hi, Jeff. Where are you?"

"Right behind you," said a voice nearby.

Dean spun round. Standing in the doorway of the kitchen was a guy wearing an expensive suit and an even more expensive tan. He had long, slicked-back hair and an ear to ear grin.

"Just thought I'd come and see how my boy was doing," said the guy.

"I'm doing fine, thanks, Jeff," said Dean.

"That's good, that's good," said the guy.

He looked at Nick and then at George, sitting in her wheelchair.

44

"Well? Are you going to tell me who your friends are?"

"What? Oh yeah, sorry," said Dean. "This is Nick, this is George. Guys, this is my agent, Jeff Edwards."

"Hi," said Jeff. He held his hand out towards Nick.

Nick shook it. "Hi," he said.

Jeff turned to George and bent down so that he was at her level.

"Hell-ooo!" he said in a slow, loud voice. "How are yooooooou todaaaaay?"

George didn't know what to do. This guy was talking to her like she was a baby. Or deaf. Or stupid. Or all three.

"I'm oo-kaaaaay thank yoooooou!!!" George shouted back.

If Jeff Edwards wanted to treat her like an idiot, that was fine by George. She thought he was an idiot too.

Chapter 7

The Magic Number

George opened her eyes. Sunlight was streaming through the curtains. She could hear voices downstairs. It sounded like her mum and dad were having breakfast. Along the corridor the toilet flushed. A few moments later there was a bang on the door.

"You awake yet George?" said Denis.

"No," George lied.

"OK," said Denis. "Let me know when you are. I'll give you a hand down the stairs."

"OK," said George. "Thanks."

George lay in bed, thinking about the night before. Had she *really* met Dean Johnson? Had she *really* sat in his house, drinking Coke and watching the match? It all seemed like a dream. Perhaps it *was* a dream.

George turned to look at the clock on her bedside table. There was a scrap of paper. She picked it up. On it was scribbled a mobile phone number. So it was true. George hadn't been dreaming after all. It really had happened. She could remember Dean giving the number to her.

"Give me a call some time," he'd said. "We could hang out."

George smiled to herself. Dean Johnson? Wanting to hang out with her? It was incredible!

She looked at the scrap of paper again. There were people at school who'd do anything to get their hands on that number. She could make an absolute fortune if she wanted to.

George switched her phone on. She added Dean's number to her address book, then threw the bit of paper away.

Somehow George knew that this was something she was going to keep to herself. She wasn't going to tell anyone that she had Dean Johnson's mobile number. She wasn't even going to tell anyone she'd met him. This time yesterday, George would have boasted and bragged about meeting Dean Johnson. But not now. Not any more. Something had changed.

She dressed, then called to Denis to give her a hand down the stairs.

Everyone was in the kitchen. "Come on, George! What was he like?" said George's dad, before his daughter had even got to the table.

"Morning, Dad," said George.

"Never mind all that," said Dad. "We're waiting!"

"Speak for yourself, Dad," said Denis. He helped himself to a bowl of cereal.

"Oh come on, Den. Don't tell me you're not interested!"

"OK, I won't then," said Denis.

"I think you might be surprised, Den," said George. She took a slice of toast.

"Oh yeah?" said Denis. "Come on then, George. Surprise me."

George thought for a moment.

"Nah, I don't think so," she said.

George's dad looked at her like she'd gone mad. She hadn't wanted to speak about it when she'd got back the night before either.

What was wrong? George was even more crazy about football than he was!

"So is that it, then?" Dad asked.

"What do you mean, Dad? Is that it?" said George.

"Is that all you've got to say?"

"Er, yeah. 'Fraid so," said George. "Sorry."

"That's not fair!" said her dad.

"Leave her alone," said George's mum. "She doesn't want to talk about it. Can't you tell?"

"I only wanted to know what he's like in real life," Dad sulked.

George's mum started to tidy away the breakfast things. "Time to get going," she said, glancing up at the clock. "You don't want to be late for school."

"Ah well, you see, that's where you're wrong, Mum," said Denis. "I'd love to be late for school. How about you, George?"

But George didn't reply. She'd just remembered. Her best friend, Nick. Nick, who couldn't keep his mouth shut if you paid him to. Nick, who couldn't keep a secret if his life depended on it. Nick, who would want to tell the whole world about meeting Dean Johnson.

"Oh, no," groaned George.

"What's the matter, love?" asked George's mum.

"Nothing, Mum," said George.

Chapter 8

To Text or not to Text?

George sat on the school bus and stared out of the window. She thought about the scrap of paper. The scrap of paper with the phone number on it. The scrap of paper with *Dean* flipping *Johnson's* number on it!

Was Dean serious when he told George to call him some time? Perhaps he was just saying that. Perhaps he was just being nice. Perhaps it wasn't even his *real* number.

One way to find out, thought George. She took her mobile out of her pocket.

George thought it was better to text. That way it wouldn't be so embarrassing if it wasn't Dean's real number.

She looked at her phone. What should she say? She'd only ever texted mates before. She'd never texted anyone famous.

But then George remembered what Dean had said about the whole fame thing. About how it did his head in. About how *normal* he really was. Or at least, how normal he wanted to be.

In the end George thought she'd keep things simple. She began pressing the keys on her phone, just like she'd done a thousand times before.

"Hi," she wrote. "Thnx 4 gr8 nite. Gd luck in final! George :)"

George looked at the message for a few moments. Should she send it or not? After all, Dean must get hundreds of texts! Would he bother to reply? Would he even remember who she was?

Oh, what the heck, thought George. She started to scroll through numbers. After a few moments, she found Dean's.

"Dean? Who's Dean?"

George turned around. Sarah Brown was peering over the back of her seat.

"Oh, just some guy," said George.

"Well – der," said Sarah. "Come on George, who is he?"

"It's none of your business!" said George.

"Ooooh!" said Sarah. "Pardon me for breathing!"

George pressed "send" and put her phone away.

"What's he like?" said Sarah. "Is he fit?"

"Depends what kind of 'fit' you mean," said Nick. He came and sat down next to George.

"What do you mean?" said Sarah.

"I mean," said Nick, "are we talking 'fit' as in good looking, or 'fit' as in tip-top condition?"

"What are you on about?" said Sarah.

"Yes, Nick, what *are* you on about?" hissed George.

Nick looked at George. Why was she staring at him like that? What was the problem? He didn't understand. But then Nick never was any good at mind-reading.

"You haven't told her then?" he asked.

"No, I haven't actually, Nick," George muttered.

"Told me what?" said Sarah.

"About where we were last night," said Nick.

"Why? Where were you?" said Sarah.

George sighed. There was no point trying to stop Nick. He was bound to blab sooner or later. It looked like it was going to be sooner.

"You're never going to believe it," said Nick.

"Try me," said Sarah.

"I'm telling you. You won't believe it," said Nick.

"Oh for goodness sake, if you must know, we were at Dean Johnson's place!" said George.

In an instant, Sarah's smile vanished.

"Dean Johnson?" she said. "You mean the footballer?"

"No, Sarah," said George. "Dean Johnson the painter and decorator. Of *course* I mean the footballer!"

Sarah started to smile again. "You were at Dean Johnson's place?" she said. "Yeah, right."

"OK, we weren't, then," said George. "Have it your way."

"I told you she wouldn't believe it," said Nick.

"I wouldn't have believed it myself this time yesterday," said George.

Sarah looked at George. "You really were at Dean Johnson's?"

"We really were," said George.

"That's who's bought The Elms," chipped in Nick.

"Dean Johnson's bought The Elms? This is a wind-up," said Sarah. "You two are winding me up, I know you are."

"We're not. It's the truth," said Nick.

At that moment, George's phone began to ring. She looked at it, to see who it was.

"Oh my God! It's him!" screeched George.

"Who?" Nick asked.

"Who do you think? Dean!"

"Aaaaaaggghhhh!!!!" screamed Sarah.

"Shut up, Sarah!" hissed George. "I don't want the whole bus to know!"

But it was too late.

"You're never going to guess who's calling George!" shrieked Sarah at the top of her voice. "Only Dean flipping Johnson!"

Everyone turned to look at George.

59

George looked at her phone. She knew that if she didn't answer it soon, the voice-mail would kick in.

She answered. "Hello?" George knew that everyone was looking at her. She tried to stay cool, but inside, her heart was banging like a drum.

"Oh hi, Dean. Yeah, I'm fine thanks. You?"

George listened. Everyone *watched* George as she listened.

"Er, yeah, I'd love to!" she said.

Love to what? thought everyone.

"Yeah, that would be great!" said George.

What would be great? thought everyone.

"OK then. Great. Yeah. Bye," said George. She put her phone away.

George looked out of the window. The bus was almost at school.

"What did he say?" Nick wanted to hear.

"Oh, nothing much," said George.

"Nothing much? Why did he phone, then?" asked Nick.

"He just wanted to know if I'd like to go to the Cup Final, that's all."

"You what?" said Nick. "You're kidding, aren't you?"

"No, Nick. I'm not kidding," said George.

"Aaaaaaaaaaggghhh!!!!" screamed Sarah.

"What's happened? Who's died?" asked Denis, walking up from the back of the bus.

"Dean Johnson's asked your sister to go to the Cup Final with him!" said Nick.

"Well, not actually *with* him, because he's playing in it, isn't he?" said George. "But, like, as a special guest or something. I'm not sure, to be honest. He says he'll get back to me once he's talked to his agent."

"His agent? Why's he got to talk to his agent?" said Denis.

"I don't know," said George. "He didn't say."

"Right," said Denis. "And are you going to go?"

Nick and Sarah looked at Denis and then at each other. Denis didn't understand what a huge deal this was.

"Well, I *was* going to meet Brad Pitt for a coffee that day," George said. "But I can always put him off, I suppose."

"It's incredible, isn't it?" said Nick.

"Er, yeah, I suppose so," said Denis. "If you like that kind of thing. Which I don't. But you know, each to their own and all that."

"Oh come on. You could at least *try* and be pleased for her," said Sarah.

"Don't worry about it, Sarah," said George. "He's always like that."

The bus slowed to a stop. The doors hissed open.

"Come on," said Denis. "Let's go."

Denis helped George down the steps. "How long now?" he said.

"What? You mean till the Cup Final?" asked George.

"No. I mean till you get rid of this thing," Denis said, helping his sister into the wheelchair.

"Oh, right," said George. "Dunno. End of the week maybe. Depends what Mr Patel says."

"Bet you can't wait, eh?"

"Tell me about it," said George.

Denis started to push his sister towards the school.

"Don't forget, will you?" he said.

"Don't forget what?" said George.

"To phone Brad up about the coffee."

Chapter 9

Push Off Nick!

By lunchtime the whole school seemed to know. It was as if someone had told them at morning assembly. Everywhere George went, she was asked the same questions.

"Hey, George, can you get me a ticket?"

"Can you get me his autograph, George?"

"Can you give me his phone number?"

And everywhere she went, George gave the same reply.

"No."

"Why not?" said a little kid.

"Because I haven't got a clue who you are," said George. "I've never even talked to you before. And now all of a sudden you act like we're best mates or something. What do you take me for? Some kind of idiot?"

"I was just ..." began the boy.

"You were just about to piss off and leave me alone. *That's* what you were just about to do," said George.

The boy looked shocked. But he'd got the message. He walked away, leaving George and Nick alone.

"That was a bit harsh," said Nick. "He's just a kid."

"Yeah, a kid who's after something," said George. "Just like all the others. They didn't want to know me before. And now all of a sudden, I'm Miss Popular, or something!"

"Yeah, but you can't blame them, can you?" said Nick.

George thought about this for a moment. "No, I suppose not," she said.

Nick started to smile. "Oh man, I can't wait," he said.

"For what?" asked George.

Nick looked at his friend. "You're kidding, right?" he said. "To go to the Cup Final? It's going to be amazing!"

George didn't say anything. She couldn't quite bring herself to look Nick straight in the eye. How could she tell him?

"What's up?" said Nick. "I *am* invited, aren't I?"

George shook her head.

"What do you mean?" Nick asked.

67

"It's just me, Nick," said George. "Don't ask me why. I don't know."

"But I mean ... I just thought ..." Nick looked like he was going to cry. "You'll need someone to push you."

"No, I won't," said George.

"What do you mean?"

"I won't need anyone to push me. I'm going to be walking by then."

"Oh, right," said Nick.

He couldn't help sounding fed up. "I mean, that's brilliant, George," he added. "That's great you're going to be walking and everything. I'm dead happy for you. It's just that ..."

"It's OK, Nick, I understand," said George. "You don't need to explain. I feel really bad about it as well. I still don't know why he's only asked me."

Nick started to smile again. It wasn't a huge smile. But it was a start.

"What?" said George.

"I think *I* might know why he's only asked you," said Nick.

"Oh? And why's that then?" said George. She knew very well what Nick was getting at.

"Dean fancies you," Nick said.

"Don't be stupid!"

"I'm not being stupid!" grinned Nick.

George could feel herself going red again. But why? There was no way a famous footballer could fancy someone like *her*! Or was there?

"Can I have a word please, George," said a deep, booming voice.

George didn't need to turn around. She knew who it was. It was Mr Parks, the headmaster.

"Is it about the kid I swore at, sir?" said George. "I can explain."

"Sorry?" said Mr Parks, puzzled. "No, it's just that I've heard your bit of news and ... well, I was wondering if you could get me Dean Johnson's autograph."

George breathed a sigh of relief. Nick giggled. What would George say this time? One thing was sure. She wasn't about to tell Mr Parks to piss off.

"Er, I'll do my best, sir," said George.

"Thanks," said Mr Parks. "It's not for me of course. It's for my son. He's a big fan."

Yeah right, thought George.

Chapter 10
Mad World

"He's what?" squeaked George's dad. He almost spat out his coffee.

It was later that day. George's mum and brother were busy in the kitchen, preparing dinner. George should have been doing her homework, but she was watching TV instead. Her mind was racing, as she zapped between channels. She just couldn't think straight.

"Invited me to the Cup Final," said George.

"Dean Johnson?"

"Dean Johnson, Dad," said George.

"Invited *you* to the Cup Final?"

"Yep. Me, Dad."

"Just you?"

"As far as I know, Dad. Yeah. Just me. Like a special guest or something. How mad is that?"

George's dad didn't reply. He had a faraway look on his face. It was either the look of someone who'd just won the lottery, or someone who was desperate for the toilet. George couldn't quite decide which.

"Dad?" said George.

"Sorry?" asked Dad. He wasn't listening to George any more.

"I said how mad is that?"

George's dad thought for a moment.

"It's er ... *very* mad, love. It's amazing!"

"I know," said George. "I still can't quite get my head round it."

"I can't wait to tell the guys at work!"

George looked at her dad. He was so excited. He was like a little kid who'd just been given the key to a sweetshop. And now George was going to snatch it away again. "Please don't tell the guys at work, Dad," she said.

George's dad was puzzled. Why shouldn't he tell everyone? His daughter had been invited to the Cup Final! By Dean Johnson! It wasn't just a *big* deal. It was a massive deal! Dad wanted as many people to know about it as possible.

"Why not?" he asked.

"I don't know," said George. "I just don't want everyone to know, that's all."

"I don't understand," said Dad. "But, if that's what you want, love."

George smiled. "Thanks, Dad."

"Dinner's ready," called Denis. "Do you need a hand, George?"

"Please, Den. That'd be great," said George. She tried to stand up. "Better get some practice in, I suppose."

Denis helped lift his sister to her feet. It wasn't easy, but she made it in the end.

"Are you sure you should be doing that?" said George's dad.

"Yes, I'm sure, Dad," said George.

"I thought Mr Patel said to take it easy."

"Dad, I've been taking it easy for the last two months! I'm *sick* of taking it easy! I'm bored *stupid* taking it easy! It was just an operation! They said it was a complete success!" George shouted. "Anyway, Mr Patel's not here, is he?"

"Yeah but ..." Dad tried to say.

"No 'yeah buts', Dad," George went on. "I'm walking and that's all there is to it. Now are you coming in for dinner, or what?"

George's dad watched as George began making her way to the door. He smiled to himself. He knew better than to argue with his daughter.

Chapter 11
Read All About It!

"Have you heard George's news?" said George's dad, as he sat down at the table.

"Yes, I've heard," said George's mum. "And I'm not very happy about it."

Dad looked puzzled. "What do you mean, you're not very happy about it? Why not?" he asked. "It's incredible!"

"You think so?" said Mum. "Have a look at this." She put a newspaper down on the table for everyone to see.

"DEANO OUT OF CONTROL!" screamed the headline. On the front page of the paper was a picture of Dean Johnson. Next to it there was another picture – of a little old lady.

"Read what it says," said George's mum. "Out loud."

George's dad picked up the newspaper and began to read.

"Top soccer star, Dean Johnson, last night swore at a little old lady in a supermarket car park. Foul-mouthed yob Johnson, 19, swore and raged at 83-year-old Vera Jenkins. And why? Because, according to Jenkins, she had taken his parking place. What makes this incident even *more* shocking is that the parking place was a *disabled* parking place!

"'I couldn't believe it', said Miss Jenkins. 'I'd never even heard of some of the things he called me. I had to look them up in a dictionary when I got home. I was so upset.

I'd only nipped out for some milk and a loaf of bread. I'm not sure if I can ever face going to a supermarket again.'

"Asked whether she was sure it really *was* Dean Johnson, Miss Jenkins replied, 'Pretty sure. It looked like him, anyway.'

"Last night Dean Johnson was not available for comment."

George's dad put the newspaper down again. Everyone turned to look at George.

"Well?" said George's mum.

"Well what?" said George.

"Do you really think it's a good idea to be friends with this guy? He seems a little ... What's the word I'm looking for?"

"Wacko?" said Denis.

"Mixed up," said George's mum.

"That's if you believe everything you read in the papers, Mum," said George.

"She's got a fair point," said George's dad. "And anyway, how *could* he have sworn at a little old lady last night? He was with *George* last night. Remember?"

George smiled at her dad. She was grateful to him for helping her out, but she could fight her own battles.

"Hmm, well. I'm still not sure it's a very good idea," said George's mum.

"Yeah, and I still think he's wacko," said Denis.

"He is *not* wacko, Den!" snapped George. "He's just a little ... confused, that's all."

"Yeah, which is just another way of saying he's wacko," said Denis.

"It is not!"

"Whatever."

"No, Den," said George. "Not 'whatever'. *You're* wrong, *I'm* right. End of. And don't even *think* about saying 'whatever' again, OK?"

George glared at her brother, daring him to say it. But Denis just smiled.

No one said anything for a while.

"So what's he confused about then?" began George's mum.

"Oh, I don't know," said George. "The whole fame thing, I suppose."

"What do you mean?"

"I mean he never *wanted* to be famous in the first place, Mum," George went on. "He just wanted to play football."

"And I mean, being famous isn't always easy. It can be really tough. I don't think people know that."

80

Denis pretended to sob. "Stop it, George. You're going to have me in tears in a minute," he said.

"I knew you wouldn't understand," said George.

"You're damn right I don't understand," said Denis.

"Now, now, you two!" said George's mum. She looked to her husband. Perhaps he could stop George and Denis arguing again. But George's dad was lost in thought.

"What is it?" George's mum asked.

George's dad looked up. Whatever it was he was thinking, he didn't want to say it out loud.

"Do you think, er, he might have nipped out for a bit?"

81

"Who?" said George's mum. "Nipped out where? For a bit of what? What are you talking about?"

"Dean Johnson. To the supermarket. Last night."

George looked at her dad in amazement. "Don't tell me you think that's true, Dad!" she said. She stabbed her finger at the newspaper. "I thought you were on my side!"

"Erm, well ..." began Dad.

But George's dad didn't get the chance to finish, because at that moment, George's mobile rang. George looked to see who was calling.

"It's Dean," she said. "Would you like a word, Dad? You can ask him yourself. I dare you."

"Er, no, it's OK thanks," said George's dad.

"Hi, Dean, how are you?" said George. She stared at her dad.

George listened.

"A what?"

George paused.

"What for?"

Denis looked at his mum and dad. They all looked at George.

"Oh, right. I see. At your place?"

She paused.

"When?"

She paused again.

"Er, yeah, that should be OK I think. I'll let you know if it's not. Yeah, great. See you, Dean. Bye."

George ended the call. Everyone was still looking at her.

"Well?" said George's mum.

"There's going to be a photo-shoot," said George. "They want to take some pictures of me and Dean. I'm going to be in the papers!"

"Whoa!" said George's dad.

"Why?" said George's mum.

"Yeah, why?" said Denis.

"I dunno," said George. "His agent's organising it."

"His agent, eh?" said Denis, smiling. "That's interesting."

Chapter 12

Not So Special Agent

The photo-shoot was two days later. It also happened to be the day that George got rid of her wheelchair. Not that Dean's agent Jeff Edwards knew that, of course.

"OK, guys," said Jeff Edwards, in his best look-at-me-I'm-dead-important kind of voice. "Before we begin, I'd just like to have a quick word if I may."

A big group of photographers was standing on the lawn in front of The Elms.

make-up girl was just finishing doing Dean Johnson's make-up for the shoot.

The make-up girl was like a thousand other girls Dean had met. She did nothing but coo and flirt and flutter her eyelashes. And she laughed at everything Dean said, like it was the funniest thing she'd ever heard. She was beginning to drive Dean mad.

That's why Dean was looking forward to seeing George again. He'd only met her that one time. He didn't really know her. But there was just something about her. Something refreshing. Something a little bit different. Something *normal*.

"As you may know," Jeff went on, "Dean here has been getting some pretty bad press lately?"

There were various nods and grunts from the photographers.

"So we've asked you all here today, to show you that, well, perhaps Dean isn't *quite* such a bad lad after all."

Jeff paused.

"We're expecting a guest to arrive any moment now. A very *special* guest. A brave young lady and a good friend of Dean's. Her name's ..."

Jeff looked over towards Dean. He was trying on some different coloured shirts.

"What's her name again, Dean?" hissed Jeff.

"George," said Dean. "Her name's George, Jeff!"

"George. Of course. Silly me."

Jeff Edwards smiled, before carrying on again. "Now, George is going to be coming along to the Cup Final. With Dean. And well, we want as many people as possible to know.

So what we're after is some nice pictures of Dean and George. Together. Happy, smiling pictures. Pictures that help capture the special relationship they have. Pictures that show what a *caring* human being Dean Johnson really is."

Dean listened. Caring human being? Special relationship? What the hell was his agent on about?

"You know the score, guys," said Jeff Edwards. "You know what I'm saying here. We're talking *damage limitation*. We need some good press for a change."

There were more grunts and nods from the photographers.

"And while I wouldn't dream of trying to bribe you, you're all more than welcome to stay behind afterwards. Have a look around the place. Relax. Maybe have a dip in the pool. Oh, and there'll be champagne of course. As well as a bite to ..."

Jeff stopped all of a sudden. He'd seen two people, walking across the lawn. One was a young guy. The other was a girl. Jeff thought she looked familiar. He'd seen her somewhere before. He just couldn't think where.

As they came closer, Jeff saw that the pair were walking arm in arm. The girl seemed a little unsteady on her feet.

"George!" called Dean. "Over here!"

Dean waved. The girl waved back.

"George?" said Jeff Edwards. "But ..."

"But what, Jeff?" said Dean.

"I thought she was ..."

"Thought she was what? Come on Jeff. Spit it out!"

But for some reason Jeff Edwards couldn't spit it out. For once in his life he was lost for words.

"Hi," said George.

"Hi," said Dean.

"This is my brother, Denis," George went on.

"Pleased to meet you, Denis," said Dean.

"You too," said Denis.

"Hello. How are you?" said George to Dean's agent. "Or should I say, hell-ooooooooo! How are yoooooooou?"

"Er, I'm fine thanks," said Jeff Edwards. "You're, er … looking well."

"Never felt better!" George said with a big smile.

"That's good, that's good," said Jeff. "So, er … where's your wheelchair, then?"

"What?" said George. "Oh, that thing? I won't be needing that any more."

"You won't?" asked Jeff, surprised.

"Why do you ask?" said Denis.

"Er, no reason," Jeff said. "Just wondered, that's all. Just wondered."

"Right," said Denis. He knew very well why Jeff had asked.

"Dean?" said Jeff. "Can I have a word please? In private?"

Chapter 13
The Final Countdown

George slumped onto the sofa. She was worn out. It had taken a long time to walk back from The Elms. Walking again was taking a bit of getting used to.

"How did it go, love?" asked George's dad.

George looked at her dad. "It didn't," she said. "The photo-shoot didn't happen, Dad."

"Why not?" asked George's dad.

At that moment Denis came in with a glass of water for his sister. "I'll tell you why not, Dad," he said. "The only reason George was invited to the Cup Final was because she was in a flipping wheelchair!"

"What?" said George's mum.

"They thought she was disabled," said Denis. "Well, Dean's agent did, anyway."

"Yeah," said George. "And as soon as he saw that I could walk, he couldn't wait to get rid of me. I mean the agent, not Dean."

"But Dean could've said something," said Denis. "He didn't though, did he? And do you know why that was? Because he didn't have the bottle!"

"How do you know?" George spat back.

"I just know, that's all," said Denis.

George was close to tears. Her mum sat down next to her on the sofa. "It's OK," she said. She put an arm around her daughter.

"It's not OK," said George's dad. "It's disgusting, that's what it is! How dare they? I've a good mind to ..."

But George's dad didn't finish. At that moment there was a loud revving noise outside. Denis went to the window to see what it was. A bright red Ferrari had stopped in front of the house.

"Well, well," said Denis, as Dean Johnson got out of the car. "Talk of the devil."

"I'll deal with this," said George's dad, getting up.

"No, please Dad!" said George. "I can ..."

But it was too late. Dad had gone.

By the time George made it to the front door, her dad was already telling Dean Johnson what he had a good mind to do.

"George!" said Dean.

"How did you find out where I lived?" George asked.

"I bumped into your mate, Nick," said Dean. "He told me."

Dean paused. "Look, George, I just want you to know, that had *nothing* to do with me! Nothing at all!"

George didn't look as if she believed him.

"I told you everything gets done for me. Remember?" Dean went on.

"Yeah, I remember."

"The photo-shoot was all fixed up! I didn't know a thing about it! You've got to believe me, George!"

"Yes, but why d'you think they asked me?" George spat out. "A girl in a wheelchair. I'll tell you why! Because it would make *you* look good!"

"I didn't think of it like that," said Dean. "At the end of the day, I'm a footballer, you know what I mean? That's my job. That's what I'm paid to do!"

"Well, I think your agent's bang out of order," said George's dad.

"You mean my ex-agent," said Dean.

"What?" said George.

"I fired him," said Dean.

"You fired him?" said George. "Just like that?"

"Yeah, just like that."

"Wow," said George. "Can you do that?"

"You're forgetting something," said Dean.

"What's that then?" said George.

"I'm Dean Johnson, football superstar. I can do what I want!"

Dean smiled. He wasn't being serious. George could see that. Her dad couldn't, though.

"In that case, any chance of another ticket for the Cup Final?" said George's dad.

"No problem," laughed Dean.

"Brilliant!" said George's dad. "Thanks a lot, Dean!"

There was an awkward pause.

"We're not keeping you, are we, Dad?" said George.

"What?" said George's dad.

George's dad looked at his daughter for a moment and then smiled.

"Oh right, I see!" he said. "I'll, er ... leave you to it."

George's dad went back in. George and Dean were alone in the doorway.

"I'm sorry," said Dean.

"That's OK," George said.

Dean grinned.

"You do still want to come, don't you?" he said. "To the Cup Final?"

"Are you kidding?" said George. "Course I want to come!"

"Great," said Dean.

"Can I bring Nick as well?" said George.

Dean smiled.

"Course you can," he said.

Barrington Stoke would like to thank all its readers for commenting on the manuscript before publication and in particular:

Emma Barlow	Alastair Hier
Amy Barton	Jonathan Hood
Shaun Butcher	Stephanie Hoolachan
Hector Darby-MacLellan	Ryan Hope-Inglis
John Finlayson	Erin Kennedy
William Gill	Siobhan Knowles
Ms Debbie Gockelen	Demi Leather
Gordon Graham	Kathryn Loughnan
Matthew Hamilton	Gavin MacKay
Mark Harding	Laurelle MacPherson
Miss K. Heywood	Caitlin Matheson

Become a Consultant!

Would you like to give us feedback on our titles before they are published? Contact us at the email address below – we'd love to hear from you!

info@barringtonstoke.co.uk
www.barringtonstoke.co.uk

Barrington Stoke would like to thank all its readers for commenting on the manuscript before publication and in particular:

Jillian Oag	Jenny Taylor
Jan Parkins	Regine Thorne
Jessica Parr	Fiona Watson
Jordan Reid	Ben Welsh
Nick Self	James West
Shauna Sims	Jade Wright
Moira Slater	Michael Zebrowski
Tommy Spencer	

Become a Consultant!

Would you like to give us feedback on our titles before they are published? Contact us at the email address below – we'd love to hear from you!

info@barringtonstoke.co.uk
www.barringtonstoke.co.uk